Molly McBride and the Christmas Pageant

A Story About the Virtue of Obedience

Text and illustrations by
Jean Schoonover-Egolf

For all the little Mollies out there
(You know who you are.)

Molly McBride #4
Molly McBride and the Christmas Pageant
Copyright © 2019 by Jean Schoonover-Egolf

Visit www.mollymcbrideandthepurplehabit.com for more information.

Copyedited by Erin Broestl

First Edition: November 2019
ISBN 978-1-7334935-0-5

Perpetual Light Publishing

More fun with Molly McBride!

Molly McBride and the Purple Habit

Molly McBride and the Plaid Jumper

Molly McBride and the Party Invitation

Molly McBride, Francis, and Dominic were as excited as they could be: Christmas was coming!

And that meant many wonderful things.

It meant Momma would be doing a lot of baking.

It meant letters to Santa.

dear Santa,
I hav ben a good
gurl this yeer.

But my wuff pet name
Fransus sum times he is
kinda bad.

But best of all, it meant Molly's kindergarten class was having a Christmas pageant complete with a stable, manger, baby Jesus, and Mary.

"I'm a shoo-in for that lead role," Molly told Dominic.

"How do you know Mrs. Rose will give the part of Mary to you, Molly?" asked Dominic.

"Well, my real name's MARY, you know. 'Molly' is a just a nickname for Mary.

"And I was Mary for Halloween, don't you remember?

"And then there was that time when we were all cleaning the classroom, but I was so busy saying my prayers that I didn't even have *time* to clean, and Mrs. Rose said I was like a little Mary."

"Um, but didn't she mean . . ." said Dominic.

But Molly just kept on dreaming. "Oh! I can see it now!"

Dominic had dreams of acting, too.

"I hope Mrs. Rose gives me the part of Joseph," said Dominic. "But she'll probably give it to someone taller. Like Sam. Joseph has to be pretty tall, right? Father Matt said he was a lot older than Mary, like four *years*!"

"You're right, Dominic. I can't be seen with a *short* Joseph. I'll make a list of all the boys in the class who are taller than me. I'm sure Mrs. Rose'll appreciate my help."

Molly waited patiently in class the next day, but it wasn't until after lunch that Mrs. Rose made an announcement.

Molly's hand shot up like the Bethlehem star.

"Mrs. Rose! I made a list of boys who'd make good Josephs. All of them are tall enough to look older than me."

"Older than you, Molly?"
Mrs. Rose was puzzled.
"Why would that matter?"

"You know, 'cause Joseph has to look older than Mary."

Mrs. Rose's face went from puzzled to downright confused. Then something else seemed to show in her eyes.

"Molly," Mrs. Rose said gently, "Victoria Jones is going to be Mary. You'll be one of the cute, curly-haired little sheep."

Molly couldn't believe her ears. A sheep! What was Mrs. Rose thinking?

Her legs went like jello and she crumpled down into her seat. Molly didn't hear a single word after that, not even as Mrs. Rose announced all the other kids' parts in the pageant.

The next thing she knew, the class began lining up at the door, and Molly found herself swept down the hall to the auditorium with the rest of the kindergarteners.

Mrs. Rose said, "Let's have the angels here, behind the manger. Shepherds, you'll come from stage left on my cue. Sheep, with the shepherds. Now, let's have the Holy Family—um, excuse me, Molly . . ."

"Molly, I said for the sheep to go with the shepherds." But Molly didn't budge.

Mrs. Rose tried again. "That means, over here, stage left."

Still, Molly didn't move.

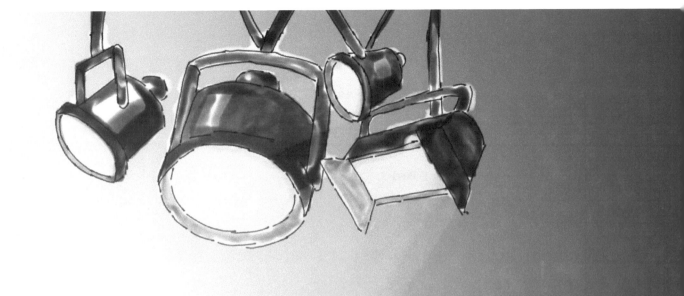

"If I can't be Mary, I don't even wanna be in the dumb ol' pageant!" said Molly.

All the other kids gasped.

"Come with me, Molly."

Mrs. Rose steered her out of the auditorium and into the hall. *Oh, no,* Molly thought. *She's taking me to the principal!*

But they walked right past the office to the school chapel.

Mrs. Rose said, "Molly, we seem to have a problem with obedience."

"It's not fair," Molly wailed. "You gave my part to Victoria Jones! *I'm* the one named after Mary! *I* was Mary for Halloween! And you even called *me* a 'little Mary' one time! Why do I have to be a dumb ol' sheep?"

Molly's teacher led her to the Nativity scene. They gazed silently at the beautiful creche. Molly looked at the figure of the Blessed Mother and began to cry.

"There's more to this story, Molly, than the pretty statues in front of us," Mrs. Rose said gently.

"Imagine a young girl who has her whole life planned out. Her deeply religious family consecrated her when she was very young. She knew she was special!"

"Then one day, something very unexpected happened, and that young girl's plans seemed to be ruined."

"A messenger from God appeared and told the girl she's going to be a mother, sooner rather than later.

"Things were not going the way the girl had planned! God was asking her to do something very, *very* difficult."

Molly's tears dried up. The story of the Annunciation was familiar, but she'd never really thought about it this way before. Poor Mary! How hard it must have been to give up her dreams and just do as she was told!

"Mary was obedient," whispered Molly.

"God knew just what He was doing, didn't He, Molly? And I have my reasons for choosing Victoria to be Mary."

Gently, Mrs. Rose turned Molly around to face the hallway outside the chapel.

"There's more to *her* story, too, isn't there?" said the kindergarten teacher.

"Yes, we've been praying for the Jones family every day in class," said Molly. "Victoria's grandma's been in the hospital a long time."

Molly realized how much sorrow Victoria's family must be feeling this Christmas.

Molly's heart swelled with so many feelings.

She felt shame for the way she had spoken to her teacher.

She felt guilt for not being nicer to Victoria.

She felt *joy* that Mrs. Rose had chosen to lift the spirits of the Jones family by giving Victoria the chance to play the role of Mary in the pageant.

But most of all, she felt determination.

"I'll do it," she said. "Being obedient is hard, but I'll obey you, Mrs. Rose! I'll be the best sheep a Christmas pageant ever had!"

At last the big night arrived.

Everyone in Mrs. Rose's kindergarten class shone like stars on the stage.

Including Francis!

CPSIA information can be obtained
at www.ICGtesting.com
Printed in the USA
BVHW021210091219
566084BV00001B/2/P